I0550645

Life is Crumbly

Written by a cookie
Translated by Jansina
Illustrated by Mary MacArthur

Illustrations by Mary MacArthur
snowflakeclockwork.blogspot.com

Life is Crumbly
Rivershore Books
ISBN: 978-0615940465
ISBN-10: 0615940463

Dedication

To my dear Jojo, whose humor and cruelty to cookies continues to inspire.

Introduction

Our lives are short, but they are sweet.

...and filled with chocolate.

My family was formed together on the 20th of December, in the evening. Most of us died before the day had ended.

It's okay! We don't have time enough to be sad for those who pass on.

Our lives are sweet.
If a bit crumbly.

I was a cookie, of the chocolate chip variety.

We begin our lives with joy. A great, big smile greets us as we are separated from our siblings. If we're lucky, our journey ends right there, in that mouth.

Eaten Alive

It's quick and painless, I hear.
We hardly even know what's
happening.

Our Baker's contagious smile is the last thing we see.

Most of us aren't so fortunate.

The Furnace

This is where our Baker sends most of us. It's a slow and hot way to die.

Humans get something they call sunburns, and claim it hurts. I don't know what a sun is, but if it can eventually kill you, it's the same as the furnace.

"You are too delicious to survive," our Baker says as she puts us inside. We're not sure what this means, but, since it makes her laugh, we smile politely.

Sometimes, this place only hurts us. We come out barely alivebreathing, hot, and in pain. There is our Baker's horrid smile once more.

Then, we are eaten.

Drowning

Very few of us make it to this—only one or two of my siblings did.

When our Baker has separated the siblings, she leaves some of us in our home.

Water from above takes away any life we had left.

How I Died

I didn't drown, wasn't eaten, and somehow avoided the furnace.

When our Baker took me from my home, I slipped out of her fingers to the floor.

She promptly picked me up and put me in a basket with eggshells, rotting peels from bananas, and papers with words I couldn't read.

I got bored pretty quickly with no one to talk to, so I fell asleep.

I was woken by the smell of mold and dust, and other aromas I didn't want to learn. I rolled myself away from the offending area.

No one talked to me. I couldn't respond if they tried—we didn't speak the same language.

I explored for a while, but soon every rock, plant, and in-sect looked the same.

So now I sit in a shaded area, and I wait for the inevitable—

the moment we all must face.

Drowning would be nice. It would only last for a moment. Being eaten alive—seeing our Baker's inviting grin—that would be wonderful.

Even the furnace sounds appealing.

Instead, I wait.

Final Thoughts

Please, if you are a Baker, don't let your cookies sit and rot.

Eat them!

Author and Illustrator Bios

Jansina has authored three "people books" so far. She hopes her bilingual talents will bring an awareness of cookie cruelty.

www.rivershorebooks.com

Mary MacArthur is an artist from Texas and Minnesota. She loves drawing, painting, comics, and sweet food like cookies.

snowflakeclockwork.blogspot.com

A Little Pot font used with permission from
www.kevinandamanda.com/fonts

www.ingramcontent.com/pod-product-compliance
Lightning Source LLC
Chambersburg PA
CBHW041558120626
46551CB00002B/246